Lucy's Lucky Bow

by Liza Charlesworth

ISBN: 978-1-338-89034-1

Designer: Cynthia Ng; Illustrated by John Lund

1 2 3 4 5 6 7 8 9 10   68   31 30 29 28 27 26 25 24 23 22

Printed in Jiaxing, China. First printing, January 2023.

Meet a girl named Lucy.
Lucy likes to wear a big bow.
The bow is bright red with polka dots.
"It brings me good luck!" she says.

When Lucy plays checkers,
she wears her lucky bow.
Guess what? She wins the game.
"I'm glad I wore my lucky bow!" she exclaims.

When Lucy sings a song on a stage,
she wears her lucky bow.
Guess what? Everyone claps and claps.
"I'm glad I wore my lucky bow!" she exclaims.

When Lucy takes a math test,
she wears her lucky bow.
Guess what? She gets an A+.
"I'm glad I wore my lucky bow!" she exclaims.

Lucy shows the test to her dad
and points to her lucky bow.
"I'm proud of you!" he says.
"But you got an A+ because you worked hard,
NOT because of your lucky bow."
Guess what? Lucy doesn't believe him.

One day, Lucy joins a soccer team.
She works hard and practices A LOT.
Lucy runs and runs.
She blocks and blocks.
She kicks and kicks.

At last, it is time for Lucy's first game.
Of course, she wears her lucky bow.
"I am all ready to play!" she says
with confidence.

Lucy's dad sits in the stands
and watches with excitement.
Lucy runs and runs.
She blocks and blocks.
She kicks and kicks.

Lucy works hard in the soccer game.
She works so hard that her lucky bow
falls right out of her hair...
and onto the ground.

"Oh, no!" exclaims her dad.
"Lucy dropped her lucky bow!"
Then, quick as a wink,
he runs out and grabs it.

But Lucy doesn't even notice
that her bow has fallen out.
She runs and runs.
She blocks and blocks.
She kicks and kicks.

She even kicks...
the winning goal.
"Hip, hip, hooray for Lucy!"
cheers her happy team.
Wow, Lucy feels FANTASTIC!

13

After the game, Lucy's dad says,
"I am SOOOOOO proud of you!"
"I'm glad I wore my lucky bow!" she replies.
Then, Lucy pats her head.
"Hey, where did it go?"

"You mean THIS lucky bow?" says her dad.
"It fell on the ground and you scored
the winning goal without it!"
"Really?" says Lucy with surprise.
"I guess my hard work DID pay off!"

Lucy clips the bow to her backpack.
"I still like my lucky bow," she says.
"But it's nice to know I don't NEED it."
After that, Lucy's dad buys her a triple-scoop
ice cream treat to celebrate!